The Caravan

David R. Beshears

Large Print Edition

based on the screenplay
"**The Caravan**"

Greybeard Publishing
Washington State

ISBN 978-0-9961818-3-9
(large print edition)

Greybeard Publishing
P.O. Box 480
McCleary, WA 98557-0480

The Caravan…

chapter one…

The fourteen wagons of the Carver caravan formed a long column that stretched out across the grassy, rolling plain. Each had a driver and a passenger riding shotgun. More than a hundred men, women and children walked alongside. A security team rode on horseback, on left and right flank, front and rear.

The Carver Family wasn't the largest caravan in the North Region, but it was well-organized, well-armed and well-supplied. The wagons included an armory, chuck wagon, children's nursery, medical wagon, supply wagons. They looked a lot like the wagons of the old west, centuries past, but these had been infused with the characteristics of those of the traveling circus and of Gypsy caravans. Most had been modified to include wooden enclosures.

The members of the caravan dressed in contemporary, rugged outdoor clothing, but of many different styles and fashions.

Austin had been with the Carver Family for seven years, almost since its inception. He had been riding shotgun for three years, most of that on the lead wagon. During that time, the caravan had been attacked four times while on the trail. Each assault had been successfully beaten back.

When he saw the silhouette of a city skyline shimmering purple on the horizon, Austin knew they were only a few hours away from the end of another long trek. Not long after, he saw one of the three forward scouts turn his horse about and begin to drift slowly back toward the main body of the caravan. It took only a few moments for him to identify the rider as the leader of the caravan.

"Wonder what Mr. Carver wants," said Marley, the driver of the wagon. Rob Marley had been a member of the Carver Family even longer than Austin. He was in his late forties, a good ten years older than Austin, and was a bit out of shape, though not overly so.

"We'll soon find out," said Austin, though he had a pretty good idea.

John Carver stopped a dozen yards ahead and waited for the wagon to approach. "Two hours," he said. "Keep a sharp eye."

Austin nodded silently.

The Family never brought their caravan fully into any of the long-dead communities they visited, choosing instead to make camp outside the town perimeter and send teams in to search for supplies. Nonetheless, coming up on a town was always precarious. While the way had been scouted several weeks earlier, and they knew where they were going and what they expected to find, there was the chance that marauders, or another band, either from within the city itself or from another caravan, might be laying in wait for them.

Austin's wagon continued forward and John Carver patiently waited for the next wagon in line. Carver was a big man, strong muscled and broad shouldered. He had a sober disposition and his demeanor suggested that he took his responsibility as leader of the caravan very seriously.

"Be great to get off the trail for a while," said Marley. He stared dully ahead. "Wouldn't mind settling in for a month or two."

"If supplies are as good as they say, I expect you'll get your wish," said Austin. While the city had most certainly been gone through a number of times over the years, it was a big place. Preliminary searches indicated that there was a lot yet to bring out. They expected to fully supply the caravan and Austin had heard talk that they might be wintering there. He hoped so. Traveling through the wet season was not pleasant.

He sensed movement and glanced down at the set of mirrors that gave him full range of view of the procession behind him.

Those on foot immediately behind the lead wagon were beginning to draw nearer, no doubt anxious to get where they were going now that Carver had made it official: they would be there well before nightfall.

After glancing quickly to the tree line far to their right and noting the flank guard, he turned and looked back at the woman and her son walking beside the wagon.

"Any word on what Saul is cooking up for us?" he asked.

Sandi shrugged and said nothing.

"Fish," said Daniel. Daniel Carver was nine years old, the grandson of John Carver. His father had been killed five years earlier.

"Okay. Fish sounds good."

"Yup," said Daniel.

The chuck wagon was designed so that Saul could do a lot of his preparations while on the move, and complete the meal once they stopped and set up camp. They traveled three hours in the morning and three in the afternoon. This gave them plenty of time in the morning and evening to take care of the day-to-day affairs that were best dealt with when not moving, and they usually spent an hour or so midday relaxing over lunch. They were in no real hurry. They usually had all they needed, and they would get where they were going when they got there.

Rob Marley grumbled from his place beside Austin.

"My god, man, how much more of that do we have to endure?"

Austin turned and grinned. "Oh, come on, Rob. Waddya got against fish?"

"Nothing. You know that's not what I'm talking about."

"Oh, that's funny."

Daniel spoke up then. "We caught a lot."

"And you did your part, Daniel. Your first time out, too." Austin turned to Daniel's mother. "Ain't that right, Sandi?"

Sandi Carver showed little emotion. "That he did."

Austin heard Marley chuckling under his breath and turned about sharply.

"Just what are you laughing at?"

"Nothing at all, my man. Nothing at all."

"You just mind where you're going, Marley."

"Not a problem, Austin. Not a problem."

Austin settled back into position and returned to performing his duty as shotgun for the lead wagon. They traveled in silence for a long while. Austin glanced occasionally at the mirror reflections of Sandi and the boy, then at the tree lines in the distance to either side of them, and back to the figures of the two riders several hundred yards ahead of them.

John Carver rode past on his way back to the forward scouts. A few minutes later a pair of riders rode up from mid-caravan and hurried past. They would be going on ahead to scout out the encampment site one final time, making sure that all was safe.

As they neared the outskirts of the abandoned city, Carver directed the wagons from his position on horseback, calling out to the drivers and indicating where they should draw their wagons. The configuration was always the same, so once Rob Marley had brought the lead wagon to a stop and Austin had jumped down, those coming up behind needed little direction. Carver watched it all with a careful eye and occasionally barked out orders to move forward or back.

Even before Rob Marley had guided his wagon into final position, security watches had begun moving to their posts under the direction of Mr. Brown, the security team leader who had scouted the area weeks before with the survey team.

Once stopped, the wagonmasters climbed down, took a few moments to stretch and make shrewd comments to their fellows, and then set about to take care of their animals. The horses would soon be under the control of the animal master, but not before they had been groomed and brushed and cared for by the drivers.

Everyone had a job to do. There was the mess hall to set up, the sleeping quarters and the latrines. As this was to be not just an overnight encampment, they would also be establishing the supply depot, medical tent, children's nursery and school, and much more. All facilities would be set up in anticipation of a *"long-stay"*.

Being part of the security team, the shotguns went on defense immediately upon arrival. Austin started across the clearing with two weapons in hand: the shotgun and a rifle. He maneuvered his way through the controlled chaos to reach the armory wagon. The side of the wagon was already open, exposing the weapons lockers. The armorer and an assistant stood before the lockers.

Austin handed over his shotgun without a word.

"Thank you, Austin," said the armorer, and with that turned about and set the weapon in its place in the locker.

Austin had already started toward his designated post, his rifle cradled across his folded arm.

Permanent security posts would be constructed over the coming days, but for now they were set up as a daily stop. Austin's position was a small, cleared area set just in the shadows at the edge of an open meadow. A thousand yards across the large field were the outskirts of the abandoned city.

There were no major skyscrapers, but there was a core downtown area from which a number of buildings rose up, several of them eight to ten stories tall.

The building nearest Austin was an office building, three stories tall with lots of dark windows. It sat at the outer edge of the city, bordering the field that spanned the distance between the city and Austin's outpost. It was surrounded by what had once been a parking lot.

Far to his right, Austin could just make out the line of an old highway that cut across the field on its way into the city. The road was grown over now, long since encroached upon by the surrounding vegetation, but the telltales were there: the straight line of a narrow, smooth band of terrain and the occasional road sign still standing.

Austin saw no movement within his watch area but for advancing shadows and the occasional bat darting about in the early evening sky. From behind him came the sounds of the camp coming together. They would be putting up the wood framing and raising tents, building campfire pits, digging latrine trenches, and going about a dozen other activities that needed to be done before they would settle down for the evening.

The dusk had almost turned to dark when Mr. Brown approached from the direction of the camp.

"Austin," he said.

"Good evening, Mr. Brown."

Mr. Brown stood silent a moment, looking in the direction of the city. "It's quiet."

"Not a sound." Austin indicated the camp behind them. "How're things looking?"

"About set for the night."

"So… waddya think? A *long-stay*?"

"Already prepping for it."

"Marley's hoping for two months."

Mr. Brown gave a sage nod. "I believe Mr. Marley will get his wish. We may be laying in for the entire season."

"You won't hear any complaints from me," sighed Austin.

Mr. Brown continued to look coolly across the open field. The two men were silent for a few moments, and when Mr. Brown spoke again, he did so without taking his eyes off the city across the way.

"All depends on what we find in there. Prelims look good. I expect there's a bit in there we can use."

"And we have a good location," said Austin. He didn't much like the thought of winter travel this far north. He was familiar with this area. He'd grown up about a week's travel to the east.

"We're here for a fortnight no matter what the foraging teams come out with." Mr. Brown's manner changed then, suggesting that he was getting ready to relieve Austin. His tone of voice suggested the same.

"You may stand down, Austin. You are relieved."

"Sir?"

"I have eyes and a workable trigger finger. I'll do well enough till your relief gets here. Go get yourself some dinner while there's still something left. It's fish tonight."

"Yes sir." He started away rather uncertainly. "Thank you sir."

§

Austin walked across the partially established camp, his weapon cradled familiarly across his arm. Inside the camp perimeter, within the circle of wagons and animal pens, were the rows of individual tents and a number of family-size tents. A handful of campfires were scattered about the central commons.

Along one side of the camp were the larger tents and pole buildings that would be the supply stations, medical station, school, nursery, and work stations. For now, most stood empty or contained boxes and crates waiting to be unpacked.

Austin nodded silent hellos and waved to several people as he crossed the center of the camp and worked his way to the mess tent; two rows of poles holding up a canvas canopy. Inside were eight folding tables with benches, enough to hold a third of the population. The far wall of the tent was formed by

Saul's chuck wagon, the side of which was open now and exposing the kitchen within. The lowered side became an L-shaped work counter, behind which Saul now stood. Food was laid out on the counter around him, and a short line was slowly progressing along one side.

Austin worked his way across the mess and toward the chuck wagon. There were a dozen or so people sitting at several of the tables. John Carver was at the corner table with his daughter Sandi and young Daniel.

"Hey Saul," said Austin, picking up a plate and waiting at the end of the line.

"A pleasant good evening, Austin." Saul smiled in his direction, continuing his work. He was spooning the last of the boiled potatoes into a serving dish. There were only a few servings left of some of the food items.

"How's the fish, tonight?"

"Absolutely wonderful, dear sir. I haven't heard a single complaint."

"Who would dare?" Austin moved forward, near enough now that he could reach the first food dish, the green beans. "Full spread tonight, I see."

"Absolutely."

Austin looked down at the flat tray upon which lay slabs of some pale, fleshy, skinless fillets.

"I don't know how you do it, Saul," said Austin. "You are the master of your profession."

"You are too kind, sir."

Austin worked his way through the line and took his plate to an open seat at one of the tables. He ate in silence, watching the dinner crowd slowly thin out. Very few came in after him, mostly the last of those coming off security detail.

He could hear the sounds of the camp settling into evening: singing, laughing, campfire chatter. It was all faintly muffled by the hollow silence that seemed to press in from beyond the perimeter.

His attention was continually drawn to the table at which Sandi Carver sat with her father and her son Daniel. He was just finishing up when Bennett came into the tent and walked hurriedly past him. He returned to Austin's table a few moments later with two cups of coffee.

"Hey, Austin," he said, sitting down beside him. He slid one of the coffees over to him. "What say?"

Bennett was about thirty, had a rugged appearance. There was an independent air about his manner. He was good-natured, but there was always the sense that he was just waiting for something better to come along. Despite this, he and Austin had become good friends.

"I say hey, Bennett." Austin pushed his plate aside and picked up the offered coffee, though his attention was still on

Sandi, not so much on Bennett. "You off duty already?"

"'til morning. You going in tomorrow, ain't ya?"

"Team One." Austin would be going into the city with one of the foraging teams. He would be serving as security, allowing the foragers to focus on getting supplies. Bennett would also be doing security. He was one of the Security Riders, riding flank when the caravan was on the trail.

"Team Two. Should be fun," he grinned.

"I just want it to be uneventful," said Austin.

"Oh, don't say that, my friend. A surprise or two would be quite nice after such a quiet traverse across the wilderness."

Austin took another drink from his coffee, set the cup down carefully and mumbled, "No surprises."

"Aw… warehouse full of pretty new clothes? Or how about a couple a' dozen cases of MREs?"

"That'd be great," Austin said mildly. "And that's not what you meant."

"Loosen up, old boy. Whatever comes is comin'."

There was a moment's pause in the conversation, then Austin frowned.

"Mr. Brown is in another of moods," he said.

"The kindly uncle, am I right?" Bennett smirked. "He's a strange one, for sure. Damn good security chief, though."

Austin nodded in silent agreement. Bennett's smile turned conspiratorial.

"You know what I heard?" he asked. "Long time past… maybe four, five long-stays back, I don't remember exactly where…"

"Wha'd you hear?" Austin asked, though a bit distracted.

"I heard that Mr. Brown was a school teacher before. Little kids." Bennett took a sip of his coffee, kept pattering on. "He hardly seems old enough. Does he to you? I mean, I hardly even remember before. Just a kid, myself. You?"

"I thought he was a sergeant in the army."

"That was before he was a teacher." Bennett shrugged. "Maybe it was after."

Bennett finally grew quiet. Both were looking over at Sandi, who was in deep conversation with her father.

Bennett leaned over close to Austin. "You ever plan on gettin' in on that?"

"Don't be crude," said Austin.

Bennett straightened and tried his best to look offended. It only lasted a moment, though, and then he got serious.

"Listen, man. Mourning period is long, long over. Being John Carver's daughter doesn't give her any special privileges."

"If she's not ready, she's not ready," Austin said flatly. "I'll respect that, if it's all the same to you."

Bennett now put on his most tired, sad expression. "Oh, dear boy, dear boy... my poor, deluded dear boy. What am I to do with you?"

"You could give me some peace, for a start."

"Mr. Carver's grandson needs a daddy."

"Daniel has Carver. That'll do for now."

"Oh, Austin. What are you afraid of? Do Brian's shoes seem so large in your eyes that they cannot be filled?"

Now Austin gave Bennett a hard look. He spoke in a cool, almost menacing tone.

"When have you ever known me to be afraid of anything, Bennett?"

Bennett leaned back and held up both hands in a mocking defensive gesture.

"Hey. "I'm just sayin…" Now Bennett's expression turned darkly serious. "If you don't move in on that, someone else will."

As Austin watched, Sandi turned briefly away from her conversation with Carver and looked distractedly in Austin's direction. It was almost as if she had sensed that he had been watching her.

Her expression didn't change, and she turned away without acknowledging him, returned to her quiet discussion with her father.

Young Daniel looked at Austin. The boy gave him a slight smile and a brief wave. Austin gave a half-wave in return before Daniel turned back to his mother and grandfather.

Bennett looked admiringly at Daniel when he spoke again to Austin.

"Somebody's gonna be that kid's daddy. If it ain't you, then somebody else."

Austin spoke without taking his eyes from Sandi and Daniel. "Shut up, Bennett."

chapter two...

Austin stepped out of his small, one-man tent just before dawn, his rifle in hand. The camp glowed faintly in predawn gray, illuminated somewhat by the glowing embers of the numerous campfires that were still smoldering. Fingers of fog slowly crawled between the tents and across the central compound.

He could see lanterns burning in the mess tent. He pulled on his jacket and started toward it. Bennett joined him halfway across the compound and they entered together.

Two women, Jones and Jennie, were already there, seated at one of the tables.

Jones was about thirty. She dressed sharp and efficient, wore her long, black hair pulled back tight across her scalp and hanging down her back in a braided tail. She was quiet by nature, but this quiet had a dark, shadowy feel about it.

She was a member of the survey team that had performed the earlier recon of the city they would be going into.

Jennie was Saul's assistant and his niece. She was in her early twenties and had a natural attractiveness. She did her best to take some of the pressure off her uncle, and was quick to come to his defense when she thought someone was trying to take advantage of his kind disposition.

Austin and Bennett reached Saul. He offered them each coffee and they returned to Jones and Jennie with cups in hand.

"Morning, ladies," said Austin as they sat down.

"Good morning, Austin," said Jennie.

Jones nodded her 'good morning' silently.

"So what do you think, Jones?" asked Bennett, a bit too loud for so early in the morning. "You've been in the city. You did the early recons. What are we going to be taking out of there?"

Jones seemed less than thrilled at the prospect of giving Bennett a rundown on the inventory.

"Clothes, kitchenware, tools…"

"That much still in there?" Bennett urged. "After all these years?"

"Books too, she said," said Jennie.

"Yeah? What kind of books?" asked Austin.

Jones was nodding in calm agreement. "Saw some how-to books we could use. And repair guides, stuff like that."

"And school books for the children," said Jennie.

"That's pretty cool," said Austin.

The remaining members of the two foraging teams began trickling into the mess tent: Madsen, Thomas, Carl, Talbot, Rawley, Takemura.

John Carver was the last to come in. Saul poured a fresh cup and had it ready by the time the leader of the caravan had reached him.

"Thank you, Saul." He turned about and faced the room. "Good morning, everyone. I trust you are all ready for today's foray, eager to be about it."

Most of the room offered a 'good morning' in return, sprinkled with 'absolutely' and 'yes sir'.

"I want you all to be careful in there," he said. "Take it easy this first trip."

His eyes fell on Austin and Bennett. He gave them a sharp look. "You two don't take any chances with my people. You have any concerns at all, you pull 'em out. There's nothing in there worth risking lives over."

"We'll take care of 'em, sir," said Austin.

"Count on it, Mr. Carver," said Bennett.

Carver acknowledged their responses with a sharp nod before turning to the rest of the group. "And the rest of you... you know the drill. You listen to your security. It's what they're there for. It's what they're trained for."

He looked over at Jones. He put on a rare smile, nodded in her direction. "My surveyor here tells me there's a lot of good stuff in there. Right, Jones?"

"Yes, sir."

"So bring me some," he told the group. There was more 'yes sir' and more 'absolutely sir', before Carver ended his pep talk. "Good luck, then. I'll see you this afternoon when you get back."

With that, everyone rose up from the tables and began moving toward the exit. Saul called out to his niece just as she reached the tent flap.

"Jennie! Bring me back some salt!"

"You got it, Uncle." Jennie leaned close to Austin, grinned and spoke in a mumble. "We better damn well find salt."

Two small, open supply wagons waited outside the mess tent, each being pulled by a single, stout horse.

Austin and Jennie started toward the forward wagon. Madsen moved up to the horse and took hold of the lead. After a brief conversation with Carver, Jones moved out ahead of the first wagon and started forward, and Madsen started the wagon forward.

Austin looked back to the Team Two group, still milling around the second wagon.

"Thomas! You coming or not?"

Thomas finished up his conversation with Talbot and double-stepped to his own team.

Bennett stood to one side of the team that he would be protecting. He gave a strong nod to Austin and Austin replied with a slight wave of two fingers, settled his rifle across his arm, and followed alongside his team.

Madsen led the horse down the center of the asphalt thoroughfare, following the double-yellow line that had once been used to separate vehicles hurtling towards each other at forty miles per hour. The horse's hoofsteps echoed loudly down the empty manmade canyon with its strange walls of glass and brick and concrete.

Jones, guiding the team from one supply location to the next, kept pace a hundred feet ahead of the wagon. Austin followed directly to the left of the wagon, staying on the concrete sidewalk close up against the buildings. Jennie and Thomas followed several dozen paces behind the wagon, watching the darkened windows and doors and the mouths of the alleyways for any signs of danger.

All on the team had strapped on sidearms before entering the city perimeter, though Austin was the only member who actually had a weapon at the ready, his rifle resting on his right forearm, his left hand resting on the trigger guard. His shotgun and several other weapons were in the back of the wagon.

Up ahead, Jones entered the next intersection. She stopped, pausing to look to her left and right, scrutinizing the scene in both directions. Above her, dead traffic lights hung low and still on metal cables. Satisfied that all was safe, she started forward again, continuing across the intersection and down the street.

They had been in the city for three hours, and they had not seen any signs of life. They had visited three locations that Jones had mapped earlier, and had come upon several others by chance. The wagon was half full, mostly children's clothing, though they had also found some writing supplies and kitchenware. They had even found horse tack that had been left behind in a ransacked pawn shop.

"Hold up, Madsen," said Austin. He stopped in front of a large window. The bottom floor of the building housed a department store; the upper floors appeared to be offices or living quarters.

Austin could see that the store had been gone through more than once over the years by other foragers. Nothing had been left undisturbed.

"Waddya see?" asked Jennie. She walked calmly towards him, her hand resting casually on the butt of her holstered pistol. Thomas waited out in the street.

Austin waited for her to come up beside him, then pointed to a shadow in the store.

"There."

"I don't…" Jennie started, then smiled thinly, "Ah."

A large dog sat in the shadow of an empty display case. It was looking directly at them, but showed no emotion. It didn't appear angry or frightened, but it didn't look happy to see them, either. Austin looked away from the dog, carefully examining the rest of the floor, what could be seen from the window.

A staircase in the far corner was half hidden behind several empty shelves that had been shoved to one side, as if by chance. The stairs themselves looked partially blocked by empty boxes and large drums.

"There," he said quietly, indicating the staircase.

Jennie nodded silently. Meanwhile, Madsen had left the horse and wagon and came up behind them.

"What's the big attraction?"

"Somebody's living here," said Jennie.

"Yeah?"

"Trying not to show it," Jennie said matter-of-factly.

"Let's move," said Austin.

"Come now, Austin," said Madsen. "That's not very neighborly."

"You want to invite them over to meet the family?"

"Why not?" Madsen gave the building another look-over. "Too pushy?"

"Maybe another time."

Jennie looked from the staircase to the dog. "Looks like a nice dog."

Madsen smirked. "You're on this side of the glass and he's on that side." He put his forehead up close to the window pane and studied the interior. "They've gone to a lot of trouble to hide their presence. That's for darn sure. No signs of traffic comin' and goin', not a spec a' dust outta place. They're good."

Austin turned at the sound of a sharp whistle.

Jones had stopped and had come back as far as the intersection. She held out her arms in a questioning gesture. Austin gave a wave to Jones and nodded to the others to move out.

Bennett stood guard outside a windowless building as the rest of Foraging Team Two brought out boxes of children's clothes. Their wagon was in the middle of the street directly in front of the open door, already more than a third full.

Rawley came up beside Bennett, cardboard box in hand. He lifted out a cute outfit for a young girl and held it up for Bennett to see.

"Check this out, Bennett," he said. "My sister's kid would love this."

Bennett hardly glanced at the outfit, his attention focused on their surroundings. He was watchful, but not overly anxious.

"Yeah, it's cute, Rawley."

Talbot approached Bennett as Rawley continued on to the wagon. He turned to the door, his back to the street. He spoke calmly.

"You see him?" he asked.

"I see him."

Behind Talbot, in the alley across the street, the silhouette of a human figure slid deeper into the shadows.

"Waddya think?" asked Talbot.

"Just curious, most likely. Wouldn't you be?"

Takemura came out of the building carrying a box of clothes. Talbot nodded curtly at the man as he passed by on his way to the supply wagon.

"I would," said Talbot, in answer to Bennett. "I might also have already sent someone to bring back a bunch of my friends."

Bennett studied the shadowy silhouette in the alley as it shifted into and out of the other shadows.

"He knows we know; doesn't seem to mind that too awful much." Bennett glanced at the wagon, gave a quick look back at the door to the warehouse.

"How much longer, you figure?"

"Why? What are you thinking?"

Bennett nodded to Carl, the surveyor for the team. Carl moved to stand nearer to the wagon and take up watch.

Bennett started across the street, spoke over his shoulder to Talbot.

"I think I'll go have a chat with our new friend."

"You're always the one to reach out a hand, Bennett."

"Hey. Could be fun."

§

Team One was moving down a narrow, heavily shadowed street. The buildings had dark brick facades with large doors and few windows.

As before, Austin walked on the sidewalk to one side of their wagon. Madsen led the horse. Up ahead, Jones led the way.

The sound of a distant rifle shot echoed down the canyon-like avenue.

Madsen stopped the horse and wagon. Ahead of them, Jones gradually moved to one side of the street. Jennie and Thomas calmly moved up close to the wagon, their hands resting on their weapons. The wagon would provide some minimal cover, should the need arise.

Austin calmly studied the second-storey windows for indications of movement. He saw none.

"Bennett's ought-six," said Jennie.

Austin gave only the briefest affirmative nod in reply. He was listening for anything further that might tell them what was happening with Team Two. All the while, they watched for any sign of trouble in their surroundings.

Finally, Jennie visibly relaxed. "Guess he got what he was aiming at," she said.

A few moments more, then Austin took a step off the sidewalk. He looked in Jones' direction and the two of the made eye contact. At some silent agreement, Jones turned about and started forward again.

The rest of the team followed.

John Carver was helping put together the framing of what would be the schoolhouse. Two others of the Carver Family were working with him.

He stepped back, hammer in hand, and admired their work.

Coming along just fine, he thought to himself. He sensed movement on his left and turned to see Mr. Brown coming toward him. *And just when I was starting to enjoy myself.*

"Let's break for lunch," he told his coworkers.

The two men left just as the security chief reached him.

"We may have a problem," Mr. Brown stated.

"Problems can lead to good things, Mr. Brown; if properly managed."

"Yes, sir." Mr. Brown was frequently confronted with such clever observations. He didn't look all that convinced.

Carver moved to a table and set down his hammer. "That gunshot we heard earlier?"

"It could be related. As likely not."

Carver took a moment to consider what that might mean. When he saw his daughter and grandson approaching, he decided not to dwell on it. He would find out soon enough.

"Okay, Mr. Brown. I'll be right there. Give me a minute to get cleaned up."

Sandi looked anxiously at the receding figure of the head of security as she and her son reached Carver.

"Everything all right, Father?"

"Nothing to worry about, I shouldn't think. We may have some entertainment before long."

He smiled encouragingly down at his grandson, placed a strong hand on the boy's shoulder. "You two go enjoy your lunch. Make my apologies to Saul. All right?"

"Yes sir," said Daniel.

Austin and the rest of Team One approached the small, downtown city park right at midday. The lawn and shrubs had long ago become overgrown, and the once neatly manicured landscape now had a wild, natural look.

When he saw Team Two approaching the park from another street, he slowed down to wait for Bennett, letting his team move on into the park. When near enough that the two could talk comfortably, Austin spoke in a jovial tone.

"Shooting at rabbits?" he asked.

"Ah…" Bennett sighed. "The idiot freaked on me. I was just lookin' to talk, maybe gain a little intel."

"That's too bad." As they continued forward, he indicated the teams up ahead of them. "How are your foragers doing?"

"Lotta stuff for the kids. Brand new." He swung his rifle around and rested it on his shoulder. "Man, I am so ready for lunch."

§

The two wagons stood in the heart of the park beside a small playground that was still open and clear. Scattered about were several benches and a couple of round wooden tables.

The horses were being seen to by Madsen and Talbot. Rawley was at one of the tables, distributing the lunch of bread and cheese that Saul had put together for them.

Austin took his with him and stood watch at one end of the park. He had a clear view of an intersection formed by the main streets that met up at the south side of the park.

Looking back over his shoulder, he could see the playground, the wagons, and the members of the two teams settling in around the tables and benches. Beyond, Bennett was stood watch at the opposite end of the park.

Jennie stepped away from the playground and started in his direction. He turned about, munched on bread and cheese and waited for her to reach him.

"Not a bad morning, all things considered," she said.

Austin nodded calmly, took another bite of cheese and gave a half-smile. "No salt for Saul."

Jennie chuckled lightly. "There's still time, Austin. Best not go back without the salt."

"That depends on how badly he needs it."

"Ya' can't salt the fish without salt."

There was a long pause then as Austin tried to come up with something else to say.

"We can use those clothes," he said finally.

"I can't wait to see them on the children." Jennie stared in the direction of the empty street bisecting the park. Nothing was moving. "Quiet town," she said. "Except for Bennett's rabbit."

Austin mumbled in agreement without really saying anything.

"You think many people live here?" asked Jennie.

"Not many."

"S'pose not… 'cept those over the store, of course. They can't be too pleased with us showing up."

"I wouldn't think so."

"I wonder if Bennett's rabbit was part of that group."

"If I had to guess one way or the other, I'd say it was likely. Can't know for sure."

Jennie accepted this, and the conversation shifted.

"Think we'll get a chance to do much fishing while we're here?"

"Don't know. Maybe," said Austin. "We're pretty well stocked up. Besides, you haven't found Saul's—"

"Yeah, yeah," she said quickly, cutting him off.

A bright flare suddenly rose up into the sky, high above the city skyline. A faint tail of smoke trailed away behind it.

"Damn," growled Austin. He absently tossed the piece of bread that he hadn't quite finished and vigilantly monitored the perimeter of the park.

"Problem," Jennie stated flatly. "What do you think? The camp under attack?"

"Couldn't say. Could be anything," said Austin. "Could be an attack, could be some kid coughed up a fur ball and Doc's afraid it's contagious."

"Or they're telling us that the foraging teams are in danger," said Jennie. "Maybe we stirred something up. That rabbit, maybe."

Austin looked back at the rest of the group. They were calmly preparing to head out. Jones caught his attention and gave the signal.

"Let's go," he told Jennie.

§

Jones led both teams through the city. She stayed twenty yards ahead of the two wagons, which traveled half a dozen yards apart. Austin walked flank on one side of the group, Bennett on the other. Everyone was armed and ready for anything.

When they reached a small freight office, the wagons were taken around to the side of the two-storey building by the wagonmasters while the rest of the team went inside.

Austin, Bennett and Jones went up the stairs while the others settled in to wait.

Coming out onto the roof, Austin spoke over his shoulder to Bennett as he started across.

"Check the city."

Austin approached the west side of the building, dropping into a crouch the last few feet. Once in position behind the short façade, he reached into his jacket pocket and pulled out a small pair of binoculars.

Jones scrambled up beside him. She looked out across the grassy terrain with the naked eye.

They weren't directly opposite the camp, but rather a ways south. With his binoculars, Austin could see the individual tents and wagons, the fire pits, and the movement of the family members.

Everyone in the camp appeared calm but resolute.

"Looks like stage one defense," he told Jones, then handed her the binoculars.

Bennett came up beside them. "The city's quiet."

"Looks like the threat is to the camp," said Austin.

Jones handed the binoculars back to Austin. "I don't see anything, but they're preparing for something, all right."

Bennett took out his own pair of binoculars. He saw John Carver come from around the back of the mess tent on horseback.

Carver swung his right leg around and slid from the saddle. Rob Marley, just coming out of the mess tent, took hold of the horse's halter.

"Let me take care of her for you, Mr. Carver."

"Thank you, Rob."

"Helluva a day."

"It has its good and bad, Mr. Marley. As do they all." Carver gave his horse a gentle hand on the shoulder. "Ask Jonas to give her something special."

"Will do."

Inside the mess tent, Saul was waiting for John Carver with coffee cup in hand.

"Dear Saul," John sighed appreciatively, taking the offered cup. "You always know just what I need."

Saul waited for Carver to take several swallows. "Any idea what we're dealing with?" he finally asked.

"Twenty or thirty of them, I'd say. Well equipped, but a lot of Old World techno."

Saul shook his head sadly. "Our way… our way is best. Better not to become dependent on that which we cannot maintain ourselves."

Carver rested a hand on Saul's shoulder.

"My mentor, my conscious, dear friend; as you have been since the beginning."

"Our way has served us well."

"That is true," John nodded as he took another sip of Saul's fine coffee. "As the Old World fades further into the past, the techno of the past seems less important."

His smile then took on a faintly devious quality. "And yet it seems that we continue to forage through the dead cities of that past for much of what we need."

Saul wagged a crooked finger. "We do not bring out techno." He had the look of a wizened old professor deriding a student who has gone astray.

"Quite right, quite right." There was an uncomfortable pause, and then Carver held his coffee cup up between them. "Such is our way."

"It is the way. Truth is truth."

"Is it?" Carver took a moment then, glanced into his cup, studied it as if the answer lay there. "It is all a matter of selecting truths that best suit our needs, is it not?"

"We choose philosophies of our own design in order that we might survive."

"Yes, and thereby we create our own truths." Carver could see Saul's increasing distress and gave him a comforting smile. "Do not fret, old friend. You and I are in agreement on this."

He spoke soothingly, gave the older man another pat on the shoulder. "In the long term, our adversaries' reliance on Old World techno will be their undoing. Of more immediate concern is the likelihood that it may give them short term advantage."

"You shall deal with it, John... and we will be all the stronger for you having done so."

"As you are so frequently prone to point out."

"Absolutely." Saul ceremoniously took the half-empty coffee cup from John Carver's grasp. "And you best be about it."

Carver smiled again and turn about to leave. "Yes, sir. I'll do that."

Austin shifted his weight from one leg to the other, continuing to watch the camp from his position on the roof of the building, behind the short facade. Bennett and Jones were sitting beside him.

"There he is," he said. He watched as John Carver came out of the mess tent and walked to the central campfire in the main compound. He stood, unmoving then, and stared down at the few flickering flames in the fire pit.

"Well?" asked Jones.

"Hold on."

Almost a minute went by, and then Austin watched Carver walk slowly around the fire, stop again, and kneel down. He took the poker and began stirring the almost-dead coals.

"North side," Austin said calmly.

"Marauders, then," said Bennett.

Carver had given them the signal. North side of the fire pit meant they were dealing with marauders. He jabbed the poker into the ground as he stood and started slowly away, walking to his command tent.

Austin turned away from the scene and squatted down beside Bennett and Jones. They took only a moment to finalize their plans. Bennett and Austin would take their teams via alternate routes to meet with the security team that would by now be running operations from the established post several hundred yards from the camp. There they would get what information they needed prior to whatever assault on the bad guys was being planned.

"The kids'll have to wait on their new clothes," said Bennett. He had a barely suppressed grin.

"Not for long," said Austin. His tone was more ominous. With that, he led the way from the rooftop down to the rest of the group waiting downstairs. They grabbed only what they would need for the coming confrontation and left the building. Leaving behind the wagons and horses, they traveled several blocks together before splitting into the two foraging teams.

By separating, they hoped that, should they come unexpectedly upon anyone, that at least one team would reach the security post.

Austin and his small group traveled quickly and silently. He took the lead and Jones brought up the rear. They moved at an easy jog about six paces apart.

Marauders; Austin didn't know how many or where they were, but based on what he knew of their surroundings, he suspected a small woods beyond the hillside to the west of the camp. They could have come in unseen from the other side, arriving by highway from the northwest.

Based on past experience, Austin could assume there were anywhere from ten to fifty of them. While fewer than ten could inflict a lot of damage, the existing camp security was well-equipped to handle such a threat without going to stage one. Carver would have dealt with the trouble straightaway. As for more than fifty, there were very few marauder groups of that size, and these were well known. Austin didn't believe any of them were in this area.

He led his team across the parking lot that he had stood watch over earlier and on into the thick vegetation on the other side. He followed a well-used animal trail that ran along the base of the slope until he came to a small clearing, passing a sentry along the way.

Most of the security detail had already gone into position. Only Mr. Brown and his two lieutenants were in the clearing.

Mr. Brown sent Jennie, Madsen and Thomas off with one of the LTs without a word or an explanation. When he nodded to his other LT, she took Jones by the arm and led her away.

"You with me," he said then to Austin. When Austin glanced quickly around the now empty clearing, Mr. Brown nodded in the direction of the animal trail and the unseen sentry. "He'll see to Bennett when he shows up." He then turned and started uphill without another word.

Austin followed Mr. Brown up to a grass-covered ridge. Down slope on the opposite side of the hill was a field of yellow grass with a scattering of short, scrubby bushes, giving a clear view of a wide clearing at the base of the hill.

Three figures were in the clearing, standing beside an old Jeep with a hard canopy. A thousand yards beyond the clearing were two other vehicles. Austin could just make out figures moving about the vehicles.

Mr. Brown indicated the woods far beyond the second group.

"Their camp is in there," he said. "Eight or nine more power rigs; a flatbed carrying fuel drums."

Austin took that in. One vehicle below, two more a thousand yards out, nine more in the trees, and a fuel rig.

Where'd these guys come from? he wondered.

"Any idea who they are?"

"Don't recognize 'em. Could be new, could just be new to the area."

Austin saw one of the three directly below them speak into a hand radio of some kind.

Motor vehicles, communications equipment.

Techno.

They must have it pretty good. High cost of living, though, and with each passing year, more and more difficult to maintain. And with each passing year, more and more difficult to find fuel.

Better our way…

Some of that stuff would make living so much damned easier... why not use it while we can?

Austin knew what Saul would say. "You depend on it now, what are you going to do when it's gone?"

Oh, I don't know... adjust, maybe...

"Their techno is going to give them an edge," he said.

"I doubt that." Mr. Brown was a true believer. He was studying the scene through a rugged pair of binoculars. "Everyone knows what has to be done. What needs saying has already been said."

Austin let the matter drop. The security team leader was probably right. This was nothing they hadn't faced before, and they had always come out on top.

"Here we go," said Mr. Brown. Down below, John Carver was approaching the Jeep on horseback. The three men watching him approach spread out so that they were standing a few yards apart, presenting themselves as more difficult targets.

Austin brought out his own small pair of binoculars and slid into position beside Mr. Brown.

John Carver let his horse plod slowly forward, offering it little guidance or direction. It could see where its rider wanted to go, and could sense that it wanted to take its time getting there.

When it got to within twenty feet of the three men, now forming a line across its path, the horse stopped.

This is where its rider wanted to be.

Carver studied the faces of the three men, the way they stood, the positions of their arms and the way they held their hands.

He already knew there were no others in the power rig behind them.

He already knew there were two vehicles a thousand yards to his left and that there were five people waiting there.

He knew that further away, camped in the shadow of the trees near the foot of the nearby hills, the rest of the marauder band waited.

Carver looked directly into the eyes of the man that he took to be, by manner and position, the leader of the group. He held his silence. His horse breathed out a bored blubbering noise.

The leader of the group stared back at Carver, confident in his situation. He assumed that sooner or later this throwback would introduce himself.

John Carver did not.

After a long, increasingly uncomfortable silence, the man standing to the leader's left couldn't take it anymore.

"Ya' know how to speak, dipstick?"

Carver smiled inwardly. Outwardly, he showed no sign of having heard the man.

However, the leader's expression changed subtly.

What the hell, Thompson?

Now he was going to have to take the time to turn this conversation back to his favor.

"You in charge of the parade camped outside my city?" he asked.

"John Carver," he answered smoothly.

"Yeah. Whatever. Simple question. *Are you in charge?*"

"That would be me."

"See? A simple answer. That's all I asked for." The man sighed wearily. "Jesus."

"John."

"That's cute," said the leader. "I don't much like cute."

"And I don't imagine you see much of it," said Carver. He let his horse finish another blubbering spell. "What do you want?"

"Now that's more like it. Right down to business." The man put on a thin grin and there was a sinister twinkle in his eye. "The name's Morgan."

Carver didn't acknowledge the introduction, as if he was waiting to hear an answer to his question and anything else was irrelevant.

"How 'bout climbing down off that sack of dog food," said Thompson, the man to Morgan's left.

Carver again ignored him. He continued watching the leader. When Morgan saw that Carver intended to stay on the horse, he too ignored Thompson, as if the man hadn't just given this John Carver character an order.

"You and your little caravan have incurred several fees that need to be addressed," he said. "At your earliest convenience."

"I see."

"Yes. First of all, there's a toll charge for traveling through our territory. Not insignificant, I'm afraid. And then there are fees incurred for camping on our property. Oh, and of course the foraging fees related to entering our city and retrieving supplies."

"Sounds like a lot of fees," said Carver. "I had no idea."

"I suspected that was the case," said Morgan. "I even suggested that very possibility to my colleagues. How could you know, I asked. How could you possibly know?" Another thin grin. "And yet, there it is."

"There it is," said Thompson.

"To continue," Morgan went on. "The toll charge. This is based on the number of wagons and personnel in your party. As I said, not insignificant. Camping fees, again based on the size of your party, and the intended length of your stay. Now, the foraging fees are normally calculated against the quantity and value of goods that you bring out of the city."

"Of course."

"Being that I'm in an understanding mood, we'll drop the fines normally associated with failure to get a permit."

Carver nodded solemnly, grew thoughtful. At length, he said simply, "And these fees can be addressed at my convenience."

"*Earliest* convenience," the leader smiled again. After a moment, the smile faded. "Delay of payment could result in severe penalties."

Saul stood waiting outside the mess tent with Sandi Carver. Sandi took the horse's reins from Carver.

"Welcome back, Father," she said coolly.

"Thank you, Sandi."

"How'd it go, John?" asked Saul.

"As expected," said John Carver. "Food, ammunition, horses."

"Horses? What would technos want with horses?"

"Food. For their dogs, apparently."

"Oh, that's just disgusting," said Sandi. Her father's horse snuggled its head up close to Sandi and she absently gave the animal a pat on the neck. "And I assume they threatened to take everything if we don't pay up."

"Seize everything; take the women, kill the men, sell the children."

"How much time do we have?"

"I told them I had to meet with my council to discuss the arrangements. They didn't buy it, of course, but they did give us until morning to gather together their fee."

"Excellent," said Saul.

"I thought so."

"Should offer a refreshing distraction," said Sandi. There was a hint of a smile on her face. "Don't you think so, Father?"

"Yes, daughter. I certainly do."

chapter three…

Morgan sat down in the wooden folding chair that was waiting for him near the campfire. There was movement and noise all around him; music, laughter, arguments, dancing, fighting. The marauder camp was alive.

A slave girl handed him his coffee and quickly disappeared. Morgan took a swallow of the coffee and set the cup on the small table beside his chair.

The sound of a nearby generator was little more than white noise, almost drowned out by the music coming from the entertainment center that had been set up at the far end of the camp. Speakers were mounted high up on the surrounding trees. Ropes strung from tree to tree hung heavy with kerosene lanterns.

The camp perimeter was lined with power rigs: cars, trucks, buses, 4x4s. Guards stood watch in the darkness beyond.

The slave returned with a plate of food. Morgan took the plate, watched the girl turn about and make her way back through the dozens of people that were bustling about the camp. He couldn't remember her name; *Janice or Janet or Carol…* something like that. He had kept her when they had sold the last group of captives. She was in her twenties, wasn't all that much to look at, especially with that ugly scar on her cheek, but she did her job and the figure wasn't bad. And there was just enough to hang onto with a little extra to make things comfortable.

He hadn't decided whether to throw her in with the next collection they would be bringing in from this latest caravan.

Thompson approached from the command tent, grabbing a chair along the way. He set the chair beside Morgan's and dropped into it.

"We're all set," he said.

Morgan grunted acknowledgement, absently scooped a spoonful of food into his mouth and chewed. He was still pissed at his second in command for the way he had handled himself at the meeting with that John Carver character. He had made Morgan look foolish. Worse, he had made it look as though Morgan couldn't control his people.

Thompson sensed the simmering anger but chose to ignore it. He looked at his large wristwatch with the scratched face and worn and faded wide leather band.

"Smitty'll be moving on their camp in forty minutes." He snickered. He always got a kick out of surprising the quarry. It got 'em every time. *You said tomorrow… you said tomorrow…* they would whimper, on their knees, preparing to die. Great stuff.

The second team, following ten minutes behind Smitty's, would handle cleanup. Then Thompson's own group would go in at daybreak and collect supplies and slaves.

"Fine," said Morgan. He set his plate down on the side table and picked up his coffee. He took a swallow. It was getting cold. He tossed the contents of the cup into the campfire, held it patiently out to one side. Janice or Janet or Carol or whatever-the-hell-her-name-was made a quick appearance, coffee decanter in hand. She filled his cup and was gone.

"What the hell's her name?" he asked.

Thompson shifted about, looked back toward the kitchen.

"Don't recall. Got her up north, right? That dirty little town by the river? I think she had a brat with her." Thompson shifted back again, settled into his chair. "Didn't we sell it off to that farmer?"

Morgan had already lost interest. He stared into the distance. A furrow slowly formed on his brow. "There was something odd about that guy."

"What guy? Carver?"

"Something different, somethin' not right. I can feel it."

"All over, soon enough." Thompson glanced around the camp, back at his watch. "Wonder where Jeffries is."

Jeffries, their head of security, liked to check on all the guard posts this time in the evening, particularly when they were settling into a new camp. After making his rounds, he usually dropped by for a cup of coffee with Morgan.

Morgan shrugged, sipped at his coffee, and leaned back in his chair. But Thompson's casual observation stuck with him. Where was Jeffries? He was seldom this late.

Without shifting position, he began studying the shadows beyond the perimeter. At first, he could see nothing, having to give his eyes time to adjust. He had been staring into the fire, and initially the shadows were just shadows.

Movement…

Morgan was certain that he saw one shadow passing in front of another. He tried not to react.

"Crap," he grumbled.

"What?"

"Not sure. Could be nothing."

Thompson had no idea what that meant. Morgan's mood being what it was, he decided to wait for more information.

Morgan continued to look into the darkness beyond the perimeter. Those damned kerosene lanterns were as bad as the flames of the campfire. He was having difficulty seeing anything.

And why should he have to? That was what he had the guards for.

The shadows looked unmoving but for reflections of firelight dancing against the trunks of the trees.

Maybe that was all it had been. Maybe he had been mistaken.

Thompson suddenly jumped up out of his chair and said something unintelligible. He took a step, stopped, and stumbled slightly. Morgan watched him turn slowly about and look down at him, a perplexed look on his face.

A thin wooden shaft was protruding eight inches out of his chest. He looked down at it, then back at Morgan.

"Wha…" he started, stopped. He raised a hand, as if to take hold of the object. When his hand was within a few inches, it went limp and fell away. Thompson dropped slowly to his knees, then fell forward.

Morgan was on his feet. "Intruders!"

No one seemed to understand what he meant, those who heard him at all through the din of the camp. A moment later, it didn't matter. The perimeter of the camp suddenly burst with life as a wave of attackers rushed out of the shadows and waylaid into Morgan's people.

For several seconds, Morgan could only watch, mesmerized by the method of the assault. The attackers were insane, coming at those in the camp like berserkers, screaming and crying out, waving swords like pinwheels, slashing with long knives, lunging with spears.

Arrows continued to streak into the camp from the trees. Morgan heard one feather past his ear and he dropped to the ground, crawled hurriedly around the campfire and scrambled to a large table. Kneeling beside the bench, he looked quickly at the scene around him.

How can this be happening?

His people were being slaughtered. They were hardly even fighting back. With the perimeter guards apparently either dead or incapacitated, and the assault team moving in on the Carver caravan, *and probably walking into an ambush*, those left behind were defenseless.

The whole world shattered in a blinding light and deafening roar as the fuel drums on the flatbed exploded. A bright, orange mushroom rose up through the trees. The heat rolled through the camp in a wave, tossing aside chairs and tables and knocking people to the ground. Morgan felt the blast of heat against his face and quickly shielded his eyes against the glare.

Slowly lowering his arm then, struggling to look into the hell in front of him, Morgan saw the silhouettes of Austin and Mr. Brown moving against the backdrop of orange and black flames, stalking their victims, slaying anything that moved.

The figure of a slender young woman stepped into the golden glow of firelight, a thin sword held in each hand. Jennie turned her head slowly and her face shimmered orange and gold. Her eyes were wide and white and shown bright with insane bliss. The expression on her face was one of absolute euphoria.

Oh my god… thought Morgan. *We're all going to die…*

Austin and Mr. Brown walked on either side of the small group of prisoners. Austin had a rifle resting on one shoulder, a blood-spattered sword across the other. His clothes were covered with blood, and there was a smear of red across his left cheek. The sun was just coming up and the warm, reddish rays felt good against his face. His smile was a contented smile.

Amongst the half a dozen prisoners was Morgan. He didn't look like he was trying to hide in the crowd; rather he wore what dignity remained to him on display for everyone to see. He had a few superficial injuries, and there were spatters of blood on his clothes.

Behind Morgan walked the slave girl. Her name was Lydia. She appeared no different now that she was a prisoner of the Carver Caravan than she had when she was a slave to the marauders; she was neither more submissive nor less.

As they approached the perimeter of the Carver camp, a security detail came out to meet them.

"I'll take 'em in, Austin," said Mr. Brown. "You get yourself cleaned up."

"Thank you, Mr. Brown." One of the security team silently offered to take Austin's sword. Austin continued alone into the compound. The camp appeared calm, quiet, unaffected by the previous night's events.

Bennett came out of the mess tent, cautiously sipping at a cup of hot coffee.

"Austin, old boy. Aren't you just a mess?"

The two walked to the washing station together. Austin leaned his rifle against a post, then carefully took off his blood-soaked shirt and began cleaning himself up.

"I take it things went well here?"

"Like a dream, my friend," said Bennett. He had been part of one of the teams that had lain in wait for the inevitable attack by the marauders. "It doesn't look as though I got quite as deeply into the night's events as you."

"I doubt you lacked for diversion." Austin took a towel and began drying himself. He was going to have to go to his tent for clean clothes. First, though, he took Bennett's coffee from him and took a deep swallow, then handed the cup back.

The six prisoners were led toward a high-fenced enclosure behind the row of community tents. As they approached the gate, Morgan heard John Carver call out to the guards.

"Hold up a minute, if you please, Mr. Brown."

Mr. Brown noted Carver's focus of attention and took Morgan by the arm. He pulled him aside as the other prisoners continued into the prisoner enclosure.

Morgan glanced once at the boy standing at Carver's side. The kid had no expression at all. He looked back to Carver.

"Carver, isn't it?"

"John Carver."

"Yeah… John Carver… what are your plans for my people? What few I have left."

The last of prisoners were led into the enclosure and the gate closed.

"As a general rule, we don't execute prisoners."

"I'm surprised you ever have prisoners."

Carver gave a slight smile. So did the small boy.

"Not as a general rule."

The two men eyed each other warily.

"So… plans?" asked Morgan.

"They will be given adequate supplies and will be sent on their way."

The two were again silent.

Mr. Brown stood stoically, disinterested of the conversation but wary of whatever Morgan might attempt to do.

Daniel continued to watch, outwardly unemotional, the exchange between his grandfather and this leader of the marauders.

Morgan hadn't missed the careful wording of Carver's comment.

They will be sent on their way.

"I'm grateful for that, at least."

Carver gave a slight nod to Mr. Brown, who turned Morgan about and led him along the path behind the community tents, away from the prisoner enclosure.

Carver looked down at his grandson. "Are you hungry, Daniel? I smell breakfast cooking."

"Yes, Grandfather."

From within the prisoner enclosure, the slave girl Lydia detachedly watched Carver and the boy walk down the path, side by side, the man's arm around his grandson's shoulders.

She watched with much greater interest as Morgan was led away in the opposite direction.

chapter four…

Three days later, the camp looked much more complete, more permanent. Structures were up, boardwalks were laid out. The small, wood-framed schoolhouse had a sign over the door that read 'school'.

Austin sat before the central campfire, which was set into a permanent stone fire pit. He was sitting in what had once been Morgan's wooden chair. Two other chairs, placed on the other side of the small table next to Austin, were empty.

He finished up a plate of food, set the plate onto the side table just as Rob Marley and Jennie came up and sat in the waiting chairs.

"Well, they're on their way," said Marley.

"More than they deserve," grumbled Jennie.

"Be nice, Jennie."

"You know the routine," said Austin. All prisoners received a knapsack of supplies and a full canteen, and were sent on their way.

"Considering what little we got from the encounter, they got the better end of the deal," said Jennie.

Austin indicated the chair that he was sitting in. He rubbed a palm appreciatively across the smooth wood of one of the arms.

"We got some furniture."

"Some weapons and ammo," Marley added. "Armorer is happy as can be. Hell, he almost smiled at me this morning."

Jennie was not to be appeased. "We spent half a day yesterday destroying all their techno."

"Rules is rules, Miss Jennie," said Marley.

"I don't care a fig about the techno. It was half a day wasted, time we coulda' spent foraging in the city."

"You were in the city almost the entire afternoon."

"We have all winter, Jennie," said Austin. He settled more comfortably into the chair. He appeared to be enjoying the early evening. "You're just upset because you haven't found Saul's salt."

"That's not—"

"You'll not ruin my mood." Austin laid his head back.

"Besides," said Marley. "We'll get something for Morgan, and it could be considerable. He's a real piece of work, that one. I bet a lot of folks are eager to get their hands on him."

"We'll see," said Jennie. "In the meantime, we gotta feed him. We gotta take care of him."

"Have patience, dear girl," said Marley. "Have a little patience."

Something caught Rob Marley's eye. Looking across the compound, he saw Sandi Carver and Daniel coming out of their family tent. The boy was leading a dog on a leash. It was the same dog that had been standing guard in the department store days earlier.

"And what do we have here?" Marley spoke with one eye to Austin. "It appears that young Daniel has a new pet."

Austin sat up and looked across the camp. "What the—

"We took the hideout today," Jennie answered matter-of-factly. "Wasn't much of a fuss, really."

"And?"

"Bennett said he knew just the person to take care of the dog."

Austin stood up slowly. "Did he?"

Rob Marley shifted back around and spoke in a faintly mocking tone. "He made quite a show of givin' the animal to the boy, so I hear."

Austin looked uncertainly across the compound at Sandi and Daniel. After a few uncomfortably long seconds, he absently nodded a silent 'see you later' and started away from Marley and Jennie.

Jennie gave Marley a reproachful look. Marley grinned.

"No choice, dear girl. Absolutely no choice."

"Don't give me that, Rob Marley."

"The lad takes pushing."

Jennie grew thoughtful. She leaned back in her chair, frowned.

"So I noticed. Why, do you suppose?"

"Simple, Miss Jennie. He pines for love long lost."

"Austin?"

"Not much younger than you when… well, when the world changed. They survived it, the two of 'em. Struggled to make a go of it. Times was much harder then, back before the tribes."

"I was just a baby when Uncle Saul took me in," said Jennie. "I've only known the caravan."

"Best that way." Marley stared into the fire. "Right before he joined with Carver, Austin and his wife, pregnant then, I think… a gang got to 'em."

"How awful. Geez, and she was pregnant?"

"Don't really know much about it. He doesn't talk on it. But I know it went real bad." Marley watched sympathetically as Jennie looked back toward Austin. "Our friend Austin deserves some happiness, yes? Even if it takes a bit of shoving to get him where he needs going?"

Austin walked casually, trying to look as though he just happened to be heading in the same direction as Sandi and her boy. He met up with them just outside the mess tent.

"Hello," he said. "Good evening… Sandi, Daniel."

"Good evening," said Sandi.

"Hey, Austin." Daniel wore a big grin. "Look at my dog."

Austin held out his hand for the dog to sniff before giving the animal a gentle pat on the head.

"Yes, I see."

"Bennett gave it to me." Daniel gave the dog a brisk rub and a pet.

"Did he?" Austin managed a faint smile.

"They took the store today," said Sandi.

"Ah…"

"I understand there was a lot of stock," she continued.

"Hmm."

Sandi sensed the awkwardness in the situation, and grew a bit uncomfortable.

She finally indicated the mess tent. "I guess we should be going in."

Austin nodded, but quickly knelt down in front of the dog. The animal looked at him a moment, then suddenly gave him a lick on the face. Austin took it without comment.

"She likes you," said Daniel, grinning.

"Yes." Austin stood up. "So I see."

Sandi hid her own grin. "Well, like I said… dinner waits. My father."

"Of course." Austin watched Daniel tie the dog's leash to a newly installed stake outside the door flap. Sandi gave Austin a final half-glance before she and the boy went inside.

When Austin returned to the campfire, Marley tried to ignore him, but Jennie raised a brow, a knowing smirk on her face.

"Bennett movin' in on it, is he?" she asked. She quickly continued before he had a chance to respond. "Yeah. He said something about it when we got the dog."

Austin was clearly not pleased by the turn of events. He stood in painful silence, uncertain what to say.

Marley was still staring into the fire. "It's going to be a long winter," he said calmly. "Longer for some than for others."

Austin looked studiously down at the wagonmaster. Rob Marley continued watching the short, flickering flames. Austin looked once then at Jennie, who was watching him somewhat expectantly. He quickly turned his attention back to Marley, who was diligently keeping his focus fixed on the fire.

"I suppose that's true," Austin said quietly. He shifted his weight from one foot to the other, then back again. After several more moments, he turned and walked calmly way from the campfire.

He walked unhurriedly yet determinedly across the compound in the direction of the mess tent.

Rob Marley looked rather pleased with himself.

Jennie leaned casually back in her chair. "You are quite the bastard, Mr. Marley."

"Quite a nice assist, Miss Jennie." Marley's grinned broadened just a little.

Austin entered the mess tent. He saw Sandi and Daniel walking over to the corner table, dinner plates in hand. Carver was already there, quietly eating his dinner.

Austin approached the table just as Sandi and Daniel were settling in. He took a moment to acknowledge them, then spoke to Carver.

"Mind if I sit down?" he asked.

Carver indicated the bench. "Not at all, Austin. Pull up a bench." He glanced deliberately at his daughter, then returned to his dinner.

chapter five...

The slave girl, *Janet or Janice or Carol or something*, stood stoically on the rooftop, looking in the direction of the Carver camp in the distance. There was a calm, cold emotion emanating from her, from her stance, from her facial expression. The ugly wound on her face was only just starting to show signs of healing.

It had been a week since she had been let go. Lydia no longer wore the same dirty, tattered clothes she had been forced to wear since first being taken captive by Morgan and his marauders. She was now efficiently dressed in quality clothing: new pants, shirt, jacket and boots.

She wore a utility belt on which she had attached a canteen, a knife, and a holster with pistol. At her feet rested a quality backpack.

Lydia lifted an expensive pair of binoculars to her eyes and studied the Carver camp. Lowering them again, she bent down and picked up the backpack. She stuffed the binoculars into a side pocket and slid the pack over one shoulder.

She looked again in the direction of the camp. There was nothing kind or warm or fuzzy about her gaze. There was the air of a predator about her.

Lydia turned about and walked smoothly across the rooftop.

The sky overhead was slate gray and threatening snow. Several inches of snow lay on the ground. The tents and buildings were spotted with patches of it.

A month had gone by. The camp was neat and orderly. Delicate plumes of smoke rose up from several campfires. Light was visible through the slightly open door flaps of the mess tent.

Two children appeared suddenly, laughing giddily as they rushed out from between two of the larger family tents, one chasing the other. Both were dressed in warm, winter clothes.

As they ran past the mess tent, they almost ran into Austin, who was just stepping outside.

Austin was dressed in a warm coat and was wearing heavy boots. He braced his rifle against his leg, buttoned his coat, and then shouldered his weapon.

Jennie stepped out of the tent behind him, a plate of food in hand. She wore a lighter coat, and looked as though she didn't plan on staying outside for long.

Austin looked down at the plate in her hand.

"I'll take that to him, Jennie."

"You sure?"

"Absolutely. I'm headed that way." He took the plate.

Jennie looked at the camp around them, and at the threatening sky overhead.

"Looks like winter is finally here," she said.

"We're ready for it."

"I suppose so." Jennie grimaced against the cold. "I've never been on good terms with cold weather."

"I don't mind the cold so much, but I hate the wet. Miserable stuff. Especially if you have to travel in it."

"At least we don't have that to deal with. We're snug as bugs, right where we are."

"Well, bug…" Austin smiled at that. "You should get back inside before you freeze your antennae off."

"I'll do that." Jennie wrapped her arms around herself, turned toward the tent flap. "Thanks for taking that over."

"Glad to be of assistance."

Austin waited until Jennie had gone back inside and then started away, working his way around behind the tent. He followed the wide path that ran behind the row of large community tents. The air glowed a dull, silvery gray. Somewhere up there the sun was trying its best to push through.

Up ahead, a lone figure stood in front of a small, high-fenced enclosure. Within the enclosure was a tiny, wood-framed shed with canvas roof. There was just enough space in front of the shed for a man to take two steps in either direction.

Morgan was sitting in a chair in front of the little shed.

The guard watched Austin approach. He looked unconcerned, and silently acknowledged him when Austin reached the enclosure.

Austin held up the plate for Morgan to see. Morgan rose slowly up from the chair. He was gaunt, with shadowy gray skin. He appeared listless and there was no sparkle in his eyes.

"Austin," he said softly. "They have you on kitchen detail, now?"

Austin slid the plate through a narrow, horizontal slot in the wire fence. "We all do what we can, Morgan."

Morgan took the plate and returned to his chair. He used his fingers to pick through the small pieces of food. He showed little interest in his meal, appeared to simply be going through the motions. He spoke without looking up.

"What's the word?" he asked.

"Six days."

Morgan held a gristly piece of fleshy meat up where he could get a good look at it, grimaced, tossed it aside. "Lookin' forward to it."

"Last of the runners came back yesterday. Word is, you're downright popular."

"Is that so?" He had little interest.

"That is so. It should be a lively auction."

"To be followed soon after by the execution."

"What the winner does with you is none of our affair."

There was a long moment of silence, when there seemed to be no sounds coming from anywhere. Morgan continued to pick through his food, eating the vegetables and tossing out most everything else.

"No. Of course not."

"I don't mean to kick a man when he's down, but I doubt the execution will come as quick as you might like."

"That so?"

"I'm thinkin' they'll be wanting to take you back with 'em, put you on display for a while, show everyone there's some justice in the world."

"That's nice," Morgan said flatly. "Very touching. I'm all emotional. See?"

Austin heard footsteps, turned to see young Daniel hurrying up the path toward him. When the boy reached him, he came to a stop. His attention was drawn to Morgan. He eyed the prisoner dispassionately.

Morgan gave him a slight side-glance. "Morning, boy... pulled off any fly wings lately?"

"What is it, Daniel?" asked Austin.

Morgan grimaced again at another piece of meat that he'd lifted from his plate.

"Yes, Daniel," he grumbled. "Just what is this vile stuff you and yours keep feeding me?"

"We got fish!"

"Fish? Hell, boy, there hasn't been fish since long before you were born."

Daniel's expression turned hard. "We got fish."

"Whatever you say, boy."

"Daniel, what do you need?" asked Austin.

"Grandfather wants you in the compound," he stated firmly. "The foraging team got attacked again."

Austin's muscles tensed in a mix of anger and frustration.

Morgan managed to keep his smirk under control. "Tough break, eh?"

"Anyone hurt?" Austin asked Daniel.

"Some."

Austin started down the path. "Come on."

Morgan watched them leave, the strange boy following eagerly after Austin. He looked down at his plate again, delicately picked up another disgusting looking piece of meat. He glanced up at the guard, who was watching him from outside the fence. He tossed the meat aside, wiped his fingers on his pants and continued picking through vegetables, all that remained on his plate.

A crowd had gathered in the center of compound when Austin came from around the mess tent, Daniel following behind him. Talbot, one of the foragers, was being carried away on the stretcher. Bennett and Jones stood to one side, talking with Carver. Jennie and Saul were there.

Carver looked as though he might not be able to restrain his anger. He spoke in cold, precise words.

"This stops," he said. "This stops today."

"Yes sir," said Jones.

"She comes and goes like a ghost," said Bennett. "And there's no reason behind it."

"I'm not pointing blame, Bennett." said Carver. He was seething. This was the fourth attack in as many weeks. "Two more wounded."

"That makes six by my count," sighed Saul. "I suppose we should be grateful that no one has been killed."

Carver looked then at Austin.

"End this," he said, then turned to Jones. "The foraging teams stand down for now."

"Yes, sir," she said. "Sir? I would like to go back in. This witch… I'd like to help."

"Coordinate with Austin."

"Yes sir."

Carver's gaze reached beyond the camp. *What the hell is this woman after?*

Bennett stood near the perimeter of the compound, rifle resting across his arm. Behind him, Jones and two others were just leaving the camp.

He watched Austin and Sandi as they said their good-byes in front of Sandi's family tent. Austin placed a hand gently on her arm and gave her a light kiss. She looked silently after him as he walked away.

Austin shouldered his rifle as he approached Bennett, spoke as he passed by.

"Let's go."

Bennett looked back once more at Sandi, then turned to follow. "You two still aren't together, though… right?"

"Shut up, Bennett."

"I mean, not *really* together."

"Shut up, Bennett."

Bennett grinned. "Uh, huh…"

Most of the buildings that lined the street in this section of the warehouse district had dark brick facades and wide, metal doors. Austin and Bennett walked on opposite sides of the street, their weapons cradled loosely across their forearms.

Bennett stopped at a narrow door leading into an office of one of the warehouses. The sidewalk at his feet was stained with blood. He waved for Austin come over.

"This was the site of the third attack," he told him. "Where Rawley took it."

Austin gave a silent half nod as he studied the surrounding area. Bennett indicated the dark alley on the other side of the street.

"One shot, from over there." he said. "I went in after her. Got close… followed her out onto the next street. Thought I had her, too, for a while, but…"

"And this morning?" asked Austin.

"Two blocks up, one block over."

Austin took all of this in. This crazy woman had hit his own group not far from there, just a few blocks over.

Bennett wondered aloud. "You think she's protecting territory?"

"Maybe… Be a mistake, though. It could help us pinpoint where she's nesting."

It just didn't seem right. Austin continued to look around them; at the shadows, at windows, at doorways. "She seems smarter than that. Don't you think?"

"Suppose. I mean, she knows how to handle herself, all right." Bennett looked sheepish then. "She knows how to lose someone when she wants to."

"Yeah… yeah, that's what I get. I think she knows what she's doing."

"Okay. So?"

"So then, what's she after?"

"She could be leading us right where she wants us to go. What choice do we have?"

"None." Austin started walking. "None just yet."

Bennett sighed and tossed a hand lightly in the air before following about him.

"Lead on, sir," he said, then under his breath as he looked warily around them, "Lead on, lady."

From a vantage point high atop a warehouse roof, Lydia coolly watched Austin and Bennett as they walked guardedly down the narrow street. She stood unmoving against a cool breeze that brushed gently across her scarred face and her long, straight, clean hair.

The two men in the street below eventually passed beyond her view.

Lydia silently slipped away from the edge of the roof.

One of Mr. Brown's lieutenants was pulling a guard post detail. He stood diligently at his station, looking out at the abandoned city across the field.

He was surprised by a rustling sound coming from the nearby brush. He quickly brought up his weapon and pointed the barrel in the general direction of the sound.

Jones stepped into view very near the lieutenant.

"Hold on there, mister," she called out.

"Damn you, Jones."

"Should I go back into town and alert the others to beware of possible friendly fire?"

"You might warn 'em not to creep up on a person." With that, the hint of realization suddenly crossed the lieutenant's face.

Where were the other two who had gone in with her.

"Where are they?" he asked. "Are they all right?"

"They're fine. We split up," said Jones. "Have you seen Austin and Bennett?"

"They didn't come this way."

Jones grew circumspect. "I imagine they'll be a while, yet. They were working the warehouse district." She started to leave. "My team is probably an hour behind me. Don't shoot 'em. I'm going to be needing them again tomorrow."

Lydia watched the exchange between Jones and the lieutenant from the shadows in the nearby brush. Jones started away then, and Lydia saw the guard give the woman a sharp glare before turning back to maintain his watch.

Lydia followed parallel to Jones as Jones moved from the guard post and through the perimeter vegetation that surrounded the Carver camp.

John Carver, Mr. Brown, and another of Mr. Brown's lieutenants stood around a wooden table that had been moved into center of the compound.

Jones entered the compound and walked over to the table and those gathered around it.

A shadow moved unseen in the brush just beyond the perimeter.

Morgan stepped out of his tiny shed and into the even smaller yard within his prison enclosure. He took a moment to stretch the muscles in his back.

He noticed that his ever-present guard wasn't at his normal station.

Probably taking a leak…

Morgan calmly took the two small steps to the front of his enclosure. Standing directly before the wire mesh, he glanced from side to side.

The guard was sitting on the ground a few yards to the right, his back against a stack of wooden boxes. He was slumped over to one side.

The slave girl, *Janice or Janet or Carol or something*, stepped unexpectedly into view, directly in front of Morgan.

Morgan did his best not to look totally taken aback, and was only partly successful.

"My oh my," he whispered, letting out a stumbling breath. "I must say, I am genuinely surprised."

"No doubt," said Lydia. The statement was short and clipped.

Morgan again glanced from side to side, then looked more carefully at the body of the dead or unconscious guard. He turned his attention again fully to the slave girl standing before him. He couldn't help but be a little bit impressed.

"To what do I owe the pleasure?" he asked. Then, "Just what is your name, by the way? If you don't mind my asking."

"Lydia."

"Lydia. Not Carol, then… and the purpose of your visit, Lydia?"

"I haven't decided yet."

"So it is vengeance, then."

"Something like that."

"It really couldn't be anything else, now could it? You had your freedom. You could and should have left here long ago. And yet… here you are."

"Here I am." She studied Morgan, as if she might somehow get the answers she was seeking from his wrinkled brow, the dark shadows under the eyes, the unshaven cheeks and neck. "I'm torn between two options. The first is to kill you now and be done with it."

She took a moment to relish this first option before continuing. "The second is to take you back, return you to face justice."

Morgan gave her a tired, sympathetic smile. "I'd go with the first option, if I were you."

"That is my inclination."

Morgan continued to look calmly at Lydia, apparently unconcerned as to his fate, whatever that fate might be.

"And so?" he asked. "Option number one?"

"I have a problem," she said, hesitating. "You see, while not many of my caravan survived the attack, there were a few. I shouldn't take all the pleasure for myself. They deserve a piece of you as well."

"Then by all means, dear lady, let us be on our way." He shifted about and sat down in his chair. He looked gaunt, as if their conversation had drained him of what little energy he had. "Make your choice and be done with it. Either is fine with me."

"Are they not treating you well?" Lydia smirked.

"Can't say as they are, Lydia. An interesting bunch. Real spirited. Perhaps you've noticed."

"I noticed."

"Yes, I suppose you have." Morgan paused to take a breath. "I'm guessing that's you causing all the fuss in town. Though the reason eludes me."

"I was having a spot of trouble getting in here. And I figured getting you out was going to be worse yet."

"All that bother? A diversion? Really?"

"Now they're looking out, not in."

"Oh, they're jumpy all right. No doubt on that score."

"And they have their best people in town."

"And you… you are here."

"With you."

"You're a cool one, I'll give you that."

"Patient, too."

Morgan stood slowly, took the one step to the fence and looked Lydia in the eye. "Listen, these people are not what they seem. I most strongly suggest that you get out of here. Don't waste your time with me. Go with option one." He gestured shooting himself in the temple. "And leave."

Lydia returned Morgan's gaze, struggled to come to a decision.

"I can't do that," she said, finally.

"I'm being straight with you now, Lydia. Stop playing games with these people. They're dangerous. Not like me kind of dangerous. I mean, <u>really</u> not like me. These people are really, seriously scary."

"And I should take advice from you?"

Morgan's tone was increasingly ominous. "It's not what they do, or even what they've become. It's how good they are at it, how well they've adapted. But mostly? Mostly it's because they enjoy it."

Austin walked across the concrete floor of the warehouse. It was empty but for a few empty barrels, some torn cardboard boxes, and strewn paper trash. Evening light shone through yellowed pane windows that spanned the top of one wall.

Up ahead, Bennett stepped through an office door. Austin followed him in.

A wooden desk had been pushed against one wall, making room for a narrow cot. The blankets on the cot were in disarray.

A few supplies sat on the desk and in several boxes sitting on the floor.

"Her nest," said Bennett. "This is definitely where she's staying."

"Not much." Austin glanced into the boxes and over at the supplies on the desk.

"Doesn't need much," said Bennett.

Austin nodded absently at that, moved over to the cot. He sat down, placed a hand onto the bedding.

"She slept here last night. But…"

"What are you thinking?"

What am I thinking? Austin wondered silently. He wasn't sure.

"Nothing, I guess." He frowned, hesitated, stood finally and started toward the door. "Okay. Let's get the others over here."

He hesitated again when he got to the doorway. He studied the room a final time. Bennett watched him curiously, an uncertain look on his face.

"Oh, damn," Bennett droned. "What is it?"

"No..."

"No? What, no?"

"Let's get back to camp."

"What? Austin... what are you... what?"

"This feels wrong."

"Waddya mean, it feels wrong? This is it. You said yourself that she slept here last night."

"We shouldn't have been able to find it. She let us find it." Austin's expression hardened. "She wanted us to find it."

"So... good. I'll get the others."

Bennett looked to get around to the door, but Austin stood unmoving in the threshold.

"She's leading us away, Bennett. She's drawing us away." Austin backed out of the office and into the warehouse. "We have to get back to camp."

chapter six...

Lydia led Morgan along the narrow path that ran behind a row of one- and two-person tents. Morgan's hands were bound, and a six foot lead of rope ran from the bindings to Lydia's grip. She held a pistol in the other hand, her holster now empty.

Morgan looked as though he was willing to accept whatever fate waited in store for him.

In the main compound on the other side of the tents, a handful of people moved about, some preparing campfires for the evening.

Lydia stopped short. The silhouette of a woman appeared suddenly from between two tents and blocked her path. The woman stepped nearer, and Lydia could see that it was Jones, a pistol held comfortably at her side. She had a cool expression and a confident stance.

Lydia chose to avoid the confrontation. She stepped quickly between two tents, pulling Morgan with her. As she came into the main compound, two people stopped abruptly, surprised at this strange woman's sudden appearance.

They didn't seem overly frightened, though, not even when Lydia held her weapon up at them. They simply stepped calmly aside and waited to see what she would do next.

Lydia turned about as Jones stepped through the line of tents and stood again in her path, still holding her pistol down at her side.

Lydia pulled at the rope lead without taking her eyes off Jones. Morgan stumbled forward and fell onto his knees behind her.

"This is mine," she said. "I'm taking him with me."

Jones said nothing. She didn't move.

John Carver approached from behind Lydia, stopping four paces away.

"I'm afraid not, Miss," he said calmly.

Lydia turned to face this new danger. She raised her weapon up until it was aimed in his general direction.

Carver was unarmed. He held his palms out to show that he was not a threat.

"He belongs to us," he said. "You'll have to leave him."

"No," Lydia said sharply. "He has to face up to what he's done."

"There are others who feel just as you do."

"Not my concern," she said, but she sounded just a little uncertain. "I'm taking him back to my caravan, to what's left... of my tribe."

"If you want him, you have to bid on him; just like everyone else."

"We don't have anything left." Lydia yanked on the rope lead. "He took it all. He took everything."

"I understand," said Carver. "I really do. But your loss is far from unique. My dear, why are you more deserving of dispensing retribution than any of his other victims?"

"What gives you the right to decide that I'm not? What gives you the right to auction him off to the highest bidder?"

Carver's smile shifted subtly, grew less friendly and a hint more threatening. He lowered his arms. "Young lady," he said smoothly. "We own him."

Other members of the Carver caravan had begun to gather, continued to appear, coming slowly out of their tents, from the mess tent, from other social structures, from beyond the compound. They silently and methodically drew nearer, forming a wide circle around John Carver on one side, Jones on the other, and Lydia and Morgan in the center.

Carver's expression turned subtly sad.

"What will we do with you?" he sighed.

Lydia was growing increasingly uneasy. She had yet to show fear, but she understood that her situation was dire.

For the moment, she said nothing.

Carver continued, now more formally. "You have committed significant acts of violence against us, and we have done you no harm. We did, in fact, gain you your freedom. Did we not?"

"That changes nothing." Lydia yanked again on the lead and pulled the kneeling Morgan toward her.

"I suppose not," Carver ceded.

Sandi Carver took a step from the circle and approached Carver from behind.

"Shall we take her, Father?" she asked.

Carver looked to Saul, who was standing to one side, observing. The older man was wearing a bloody apron and was using it to absently wipe blood from his hands. Saul shook his head negatively, albeit reluctantly.

With that, Carver spoke to his daughter while turning his gaze back to Lydia.

"It would appear not, my daughter. The larders are full. We do not take more than we can use."

"Perhaps a party," she pleaded, near crestfallen. "A celebration… the attacks are ended."

"We will celebrate," answered her father. "But we have all the fish that we can use."

Austin and Bennett stepped into the circle. Carver gave them a "good work" nod. Austin took a step closer to Lydia. He stopped, stood in motionless silence.

Jones continued to wait several paces behind Lydia.

"We are a patient people," said Carver, "but I grow weary of this."

"Then let me go." Lydia yanked hard on the lead. "With this."

Enough is enough.

Carver spoke precisely. "He is staying with us. Of that, let there be no mistake. The only issue remaining before us is the question of your future."

"That is of no concern to me."

"Your concern, or lack thereof, means nothing to us," Carver responded with increasing impatience. "We might be willing to take into account that no one has been killed. I can assume that was intentional?"

Lydia said nothing. Her stance and expression made it clear that she had nothing more to say.

Carver now appeared to be bored with it all. "We are done with this, then," he concluded.

From near Lydia's feet, Morgan let out a morbid chuckle.

"My dear… it looks to be Option One after all."

There was no change in her expression. With only the slightest movement, and without taking her eyes from Carver, she shifted her pistol and pulled the trigger.

The loud, booming gunshot echoed hollowly in the silence of the camp. The sound reverberated away from the compound in all directions, fading into the distance.

A cloud of pink and white burst from the side of Morgan's head, seemed to hang suspended in the air.

Lydia, still looking with dead calm at Carver, held on the rope lead for several seconds. When she finally let go, the body of Morgan crumpled to her feet.

Austin and Jones both raised their weapons and targeted Lydia.

Carver looked dispassionately at Lydia. "Oh, dear," he said.

Lydia tossed her pistol onto the ground in front of her.

epilog…

It was a bright, clear day. The camp had been struck, the buildings were gone, the tents were packed up and put away.

The wagons formed a circle in the center of the clearing that had been their home for the last four months. Austin and Sandi stood next to the lead wagon, holding hands, Daniel beside them absently gnawing on a stick of jerky.

A number of men and women on horseback were already starting out of the site. Carver guided his horse forward and turned about to face the caravan.

"Let's move out," he called.

Those on foot started forward, following Carver out of the clearing.

Marley called down to Austin. "Come on now, buddy."

Austin and Sandi held hands a moment more. They pulled apart then and Austin climbed aboard. Looking back down at her, they shared a smile. She laid a hand on her belly. She was just beginning to show signs of being pregnant.

Austin looked at Marley. "Well?" he urged.

"Well nothing, let's do this."

The fourteen wagons of the Carver caravan traveled in column across the grassy, rolling terrain. More than a hundred men, women and children walked alongside the wagons.

Marley was driving the lead wagon. Beside him, Austin rode shotgun.

Sandi Carver and young Daniel walked beside the lead wagon. When Sandi glanced up, she saw Austin

looking down at her. The two shared a
furtive smile, then Sandi pointedly
turned away and focused on the way
ahead.

Austin grinned and turned his
attention back to his duty. He ignored
the faint smirk that appeared and then
faded from Marley's face.

"Gotta tell ya', Austin," Marley said in
a casual, conversational tone. "In spite
of everything, this is without a doubt the
best *long-stay* I can remember."

"Yeah. Yeah... 'spect so."

"Yeah, that too," Marley said with a
light chuckle.

"Yeah... 'spect so..."

The Carver caravan had spent the
entire winter camped outside the city.
The members of the tribe were rested,
healthy, and ready to move on after the
long-stay. The caravan was well-
stocked. The abandoned city had
provided them with all the supplies they
needed, including Saul's salt.

Something in the distance caught Austin's attention. Without drawing notice, he turned his head slightly and studied the wooded shadows at the outer edges of a grove of trees in the distance.

He saw it, then. A figure silhouetted against the trees.

It was Lydia. She stood stoically, watching the Carver caravan as it moved slowly across the open plain.

Austin relaxed, though he continued to keep an eye on her.

There was nothing threatening. She simply stood there… observing.

Austin's calm gaze drifted from Lydia back to Sandi, then forward.

The caravan rolled on, the sound of wheels turning on their axles, wood striking wood, canvas slapping.

We do not take more than we can use…

… end

www.ingramcontent.com/pod-product-compliance
Lightning Source LLC
Chambersburg PA
CBHW051844170626
46807CB00003B/1345